Safe!

Oh no!
The baby swans are missing!

Aurora looks in the field.
No baby swans.

Flora looks in the bushes.
No baby swans.

Fauna looks in the tree.
No baby swans.

Merryweather looks in the pond.
No baby swans.

Here they are!
They are in the grass.

The baby swans are safe!